Dora's Costume Party!

by Christine Ricci
illustrated by Zina Saunders

SCHOLASTIC INC.

New York Toronto London Auckland Sydney
Mexico City New Delhi Hong Kong Buenos Aires

¡Hola! I'm Dora! Today is Halloween. My favorite thing about Halloween is getting dressed up in a costume. We're having a Halloween costume party at my house, and everyone is getting ready. But Boots can't decide what costume to wear.

Boots might want to dress up as a superhero who rescues anyone who needs help. Or he could be a baseball player who can hit the ball over the fence and win the game!

Or maybe he'll be a clown who does tricks in the circus. Boots can't decide, and it's almost time for the party!

Look! There's Tico! Do you know what Tico wants to be for Halloween? Yeah, a cowboy! Tico is pretending that he's a cowboy who rides a horse through the desert! Wow! What a great costume!

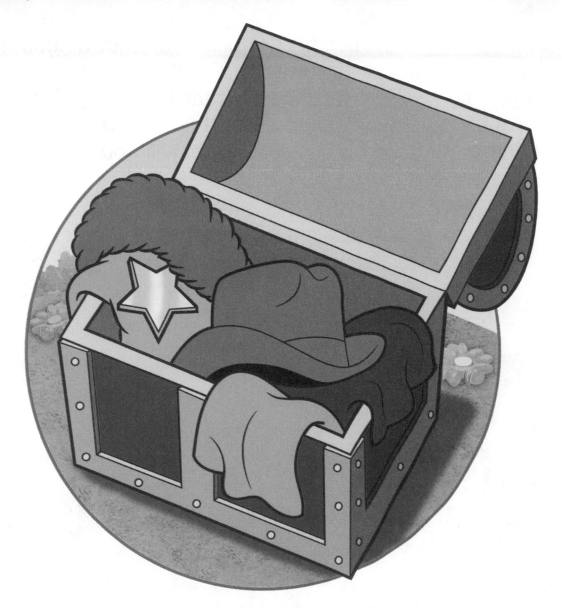

But Tico is missing part of his costume. Let's help him look in the costume box. Do you see a cowboy hat? Now we just need to find a star badge. Great! Tico's costume is finished. We'll see Tico at the party.

Benny's still working on his costume too. What do you think Benny wants to be for Halloween? *Sí*, a slice of pizza! That's a really yummy costume idea. Benny's favorite kind of pizza has pepperoni, peppers, and cheese on it! But he needs help to put these ingredients on his pizza costume. Will you help?

Benny can use red circles for pepperoni. Let's look for five red circles. The green squares look like peppers. Will you find four green squares for him? And the yellow rectangles can be cheese. Do you see eight yellow rectangles? *¡Excelente!* Thanks for helping Benny get his costume ready!

Guess what Isa wants to be for Halloween. Isa's going to be the most graceful ballerina ever! She'll use her ballet slippers to stand on her tiptoes, twirl around, and jump in the air.

There's my cousin Diego. He's going to dress up like a deep-sea diver. A deep-sea diver explores the ocean looking at fish and animals. Diego already has on his special diving suit, but he still needs to find his flippers and a swimming mask. Do you see them?

Seeing all these great costumes gave Boots an idea for his Halloween costume. But it's a surprise! Boots promises that we'll see his Halloween costume at the party. *¡Vámonos!* We're almost at my house!

Look! My baby sister and brother are dressed in their costumes.

Can you guess what my baby sister is for Halloween? *Sí, una fresa.* Strawberries are her favorite fruit!

Can you guess what my baby brother's costume is?
Yes, he's dressed as *las uvas*. He loves grapes.

The babies are so cute in their costumes! Now it's my turn to get ready. I'm wearing a flower costume. But my costume is missing two petals. To figure out where the missing ones go, let's look at the colors of the petals: yellow, red, orange.

It's a pattern. Do you see where the red petal belongs? Where does the orange petal go?

Let's decorate *mi casa*! First *Papi* needs help with the cake. Will you find two triangles for the pumpkin's eyes? *¡Gracias!* *Abuela* needs help finding the balloons. Do you see five orange balloons? Let's count them in Spanish. *¡Uno, dos, tres, cuatro, cinco!* Now, let's help *Mami* look for ten apples to go inside the ten goody bags!

Oh! I think I hear someone at the door.

The guests are here! There's Isa, the graceful ballerina. Tico, the cowboy, is riding his trusty horse. Benny's pizza costume looks delicious! And Diego really looks like a deep-sea diver.

Here he is! But what is Boots's Halloween costume?

Oooooh! Boots couldn't decide on just one thing for his Halloween costume. So he decided to wear all of his favorite costumes.

He's a superhero-baseball player-clown! What a cool costume!

Everyone has such great Halloween costumes. Thanks for helping us get ready for the party. We did it! Happy Halloween!

'WELL-LOVED TALES'

Sleeping Beauty

A LADYBIRD 'EASY-READING' BOOK

retold by VERA SOUTHGATE, M.A., B.Com.

with illustrations by
ERIC WINTER

Ladybird Books Loughborough

SLEEPING BEAUTY

Once upon a time there lived a King and Queen who were very happy, except for one thing. They both longed to have children but they had none. Every day they said to each other, "Ah, if only we had a child!"

Now it happened one day, when the Queen had been bathing, a frog crept out of the water and spoke to her. It said, "Your wish shall come true. Before a year has gone by, you shall have a daughter."

The Queen was delighted and she hurried to tell her husband the good news.

Within the year, it happened as the frog had said. A baby daughter was born to the King and Queen and they were filled with joy. The child was so pretty that everyone who came to see her cried, "What a beautiful baby!"

The King was so proud of his baby daughter that he ordered a wonderful christening feast to be prepared.

The King invited all his friends to the feast, as well as kings, queens, princes and princesses from other kingdoms.

The King wanted the good fairies to be godmothers to his daughter. Now there were thirteen fairies in his kingdom, but one was very old and no-one had seen her for many years. As the King only had twelve golden plates, he invited just twelve of the fairies to come to the christening feast. The old fairy was not invited.

When the christening feast was over, the good fairies went up to the princess, to give her their magic gifts.

The first fairy said, "You shall have a beautiful face."

The second fairy said, "You shall think beautiful thoughts."

The third fairy said, "You shall be kind and loving."

The fourth fairy said, "You shall dance like a fairy."

The fifth fairy said, "You shall sing like a nightingale."

When eleven of the fairies had given their gifts, the baby had been promised everything in the world one could wish for.

At that moment, the thirteenth fairy suddenly arrived. She was furious because the King had not invited her to the feast. Pointing to the baby, she cried in a loud voice, "When the King's daughter is fifteen years old, she shall prick herself with a spindle and fall down dead."

Without another word she rushed out of the palace.

All the people at the christening feast fell back in horror, when they heard the words of the wicked fairy. The Queen began to cry and the King did not know how to comfort her.

Then the twelfth good fairy, who had not yet given the baby her gift, stepped forward.

"Do not weep, Oh, Queen!" she said, "I shall do what I can to help. I cannot undo the evil spell of the wicked fairy, but I can soften it a little."

"The Princess will prick herself with a spindle," went on the twelfth fairy, "but she shall not die. She will fall into a deep sleep that will last for a hundred years."

The King thanked the fairy for her kindness. Yet he did not want to think of his child sleeping for one hundred years. So he gave orders that every spindle in the whole kingdom should be burned. His messengers were sent to every town and village to see that this was done.

As time went by, the baby Princess grew into a lovely girl. All the gifts that the good fairies had promised, were hers.

She had a beautiful face and she thought beautiful thoughts. She danced like a fairy and she sang like a nightingale.

She was happy and gay, so that all who were near her were happy too. She was kind and loving, so that all who knew her, loved her.

The King and Queen found great joy in their daughter.

Now it happened that on the very day when the Princess was fifteen years old, the King and Queen were not at home.

To amuse herself, the girl wandered all over the palace. She opened the doors of dozens of rooms that she had never seen before.

At last she came to an old tower. She climbed up the narrow, winding staircase and found a little door at the top. She turned the rusty key in the lock and the door opened.

There, in a little room, sat an old woman at her spinning wheel busily spinning flax.

"Good day, good dame," said the Princess. "What are you doing?"

"I am spinning, my child," replied the old woman.

"Oh, how wonderful!" cried the Princess. "Please let me try."

No sooner had the Princess touched the spindle than the words of the wicked fairy came true. She pricked her finger.

As soon as she felt the prick of the spindle, the Princess fell upon the bed, in a deep sleep.

The old woman fell asleep upon her chair. And every other living creature within the palace also fell asleep.

At that very moment, the King and Queen had returned home for their daughter's birthday. They fell asleep in the great hall of the palace. The lords and ladies who were with them, fell asleep nearby.

In the stables, the horses fell asleep. In the courtyard, the dogs stopped barking and fell asleep. On the roof, the pigeons stopped cooing and fell asleep. On the palace walls, the flies stopped crawling and fell asleep.

In the kitchen, the fire died out and the meat stopped cooking. The cook had been just about to box the scullery boy's ears, because of something he had forgotten to do. But the cook fell asleep and so did the scullery boy.

The whole palace became silent. Not a living creature moved. The wind dropped and, on the trees in the palace garden, not a leaf stirred.

A hedge of thorns sprang up around the palace and its gardens. Every year, the hedge grew higher and higher, and thicker and thicker. At last it grew so tall that it almost hid the palace. Only the flag and the topmost towers could be seen above it.

The story of the beautiful princess who lay asleep, spread throughout the kingdom and far beyond. She became known as Sleeping Beauty.

From time to time many princes who had heard of her beauty, journeyed to the palace, hoping to waken her. But the thorn hedge grew so thickly that none of the princes could force his way through it. Each one who tried, found his hands and face torn and bleeding and he had to give up.

After many years, another king's son visited the kingdom of Sleeping Beauty. An old man told this Prince a tale which his grandfather had told him.

The tale was of a castle, hidden behind the thick hedge of thorns that grew nearby. In the castle a beautiful princess, known as Sleeping Beauty, lay asleep. Her mother and father, and all the people in the palace, also lay fast asleep. It was said that they had all been sleeping for one hundred years.

When the Prince heard the old man's tale, he said, "I must see this beautiful princess and try to waken her."

"Ah! but wait, sir!" cried the old man, "you do not know the dangers. My grandfather told me that, in years gone by, many young princes tried to break through the hedge. None could do it. Each one was badly wounded by the cruel thorns."

"I am not afraid," replied the Prince. "I must try to see this lovely princess."

Now it happened that the very day on which the Prince arrived, was exactly one hundred years after Sleeping Beauty had fallen asleep. The evil spell of the wicked fairy had come to its end.

As the Prince began to push against the hedge of thorns, every thorn turned into a lovely rose. The hedge opened, of its own accord, to let him pass through. And, as he passed, the hedge of roses gently closed again behind him.

In this way, in great wonder, the Prince made his way right through the hedge.

At last he came to the courtyard of the castle, where the dogs lay sleeping. He looked up at the roof of the palace and there the pigeons sat asleep, with their heads tucked under their wings. The Prince wandered into the stables and there he found the horses, all standing asleep.

Not a sound was to be heard in the whole of the palace.

Next the Prince went into the palace kitchen. There he saw the flies asleep on the wall. The fire was out and the meat was half cooked.

The cook stood asleep, with his hand stretched out towards the scullery boy. The scullery boy had fallen asleep, just as he was running away from the cook.

The kitchen maid was sitting asleep at the table, ready to pluck a chicken for dinner.

The Prince walked further into the silent palace, until at last he came to the great hall. There the King and Queen sat asleep on their thrones. Around them their lords and ladies sat sleeping.

All was so quiet that the Prince felt he should tiptoe, in case he wakened the sleepers.

He wandered along corridors and up flights of stairs. He looked in all the rooms he could find, but nowhere did he see Sleeping Beauty.

At length the Prince came to the foot of the highest tower. He began to climb the narrow, winding staircase. When he reached the door at the top, he pushed it gently open and stepped into the small room.

There, on the bed, lay sleeping the most beautiful maiden he had ever seen. The Prince could not take his eyes from her face.

For a long time, he looked at her in wonder, then he bent over and gave her a kiss.

At that moment, Sleeping Beauty opened her eyes and gave the Prince a wonderful smile. Then she sat up, quite wide awake.

The Prince gave her his hand and she stood up. Together they went down the narrow, winding staircase, along the corridors, down the main staircase, and into the great hall.

At that moment, the King and Queen awoke from their sleep. They were overjoyed to see their daughter awake and well, and they welcomed the Prince who had broken the spell.

Then the lords and ladies in the great hall awakened, and the whole palace began to stir.

In the kitchen, the fire began to burn and the meat began to cook. The maid began to pluck the chicken. The scullery boy ran off before the cook could box his ears.

In the courtyard, the dogs awakened and began to bark. In the stables, the horses were stirring and the pigeons on the roof awakened and flew away.

The palace had come to life again after its sleep of one hundred years. Everyone in the palace was both astonished and delighted.

Around the palace, the high hedge vanished.

A wonderful wedding feast was prepared. The handsome Prince was married to Sleeping Beauty and they lived happily ever after.